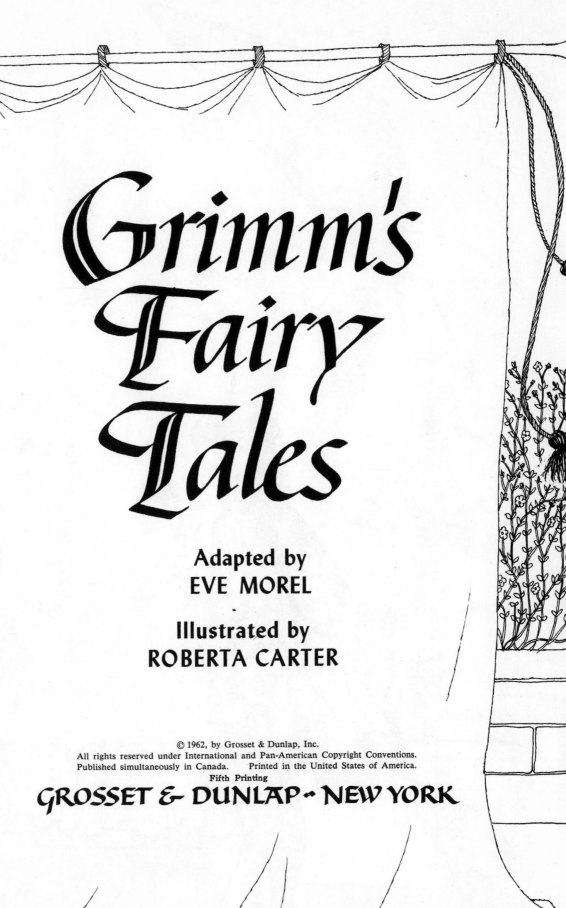

Grimm's Fairy Tales

Adapted by
EVE MOREL

Illustrated by
ROBERTA CARTER

Fifth Printing
GROSSET & DUNLAP · NEW YORK

Sleeping Beauty

ONCE upon a time there lived a King and Queen who had no children. Not a day passed that the Queen did not say, "If only we had a child!"

One day, as the Queen was walking beside the river, a little fish lifted its head out of the water and said, "Dear Queen, your wish shall be fulfilled. You will soon have a daughter."

What the fish foretold came true. The Queen had a little girl who was so beautiful that the King never tired of looking at her, and in his great joy he ordered a magnificent feast to be prepared. He invited all his relatives, friends and neighbors, and the fairies as well, in order that they might be kind and good to his little daughter, and bless her.

Now there were thirteen fairies in his kingdom, but since the King had only twelve golden plates for them to eat from, one of the fairies was not invited and had to stay at home. All the others came, and after the feast was over, they gave their best gifts to the little Princess: one gave her virtue, another beauty, and a third riches, and so on, till she had everything she could ever wish for or need.

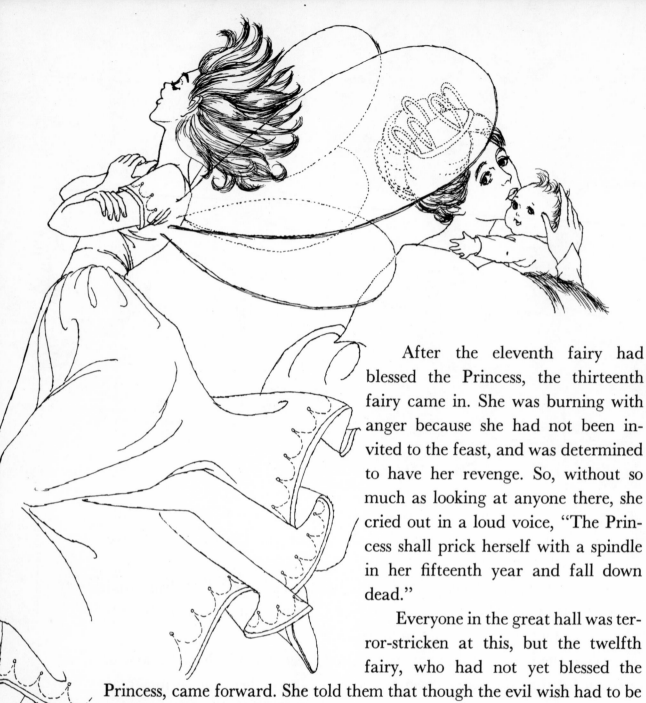

After the eleventh fairy had blessed the Princess, the thirteenth fairy came in. She was burning with anger because she had not been invited to the feast, and was determined to have her revenge. So, without so much as looking at anyone there, she cried out in a loud voice, "The Princess shall prick herself with a spindle in her fifteenth year and fall down dead."

Everyone in the great hall was terror-stricken at this, but the twelfth fairy, who had not yet blessed the Princess, came forward. She told them that though the evil wish had to be fulfilled, she could soften it.

"The Princess shall not die," said the twelfth fairy, "but shall fall into a deep sleep that will last a hundred years."

The King, however, hoping to save his dear child from the dreadful misfortune, ordered all the spindles in the kingdom destroyed at once.

Meanwhile, as time passed, all the fairies' gifts were fulfilled. The Princess was so beautiful, so virtuous, so kind and wise, that she was loved by everyone who saw her.

Now it happened that on the very day that the Princess was fifteen years old, the King and Queen were not at home, and she was alone in the palace. She spent the time wandering through the rooms by herself, looking at everything, until she came to an old tower. A winding staircase led to a little door in the tower, and in the door was a golden key. When the Princess turned the key, the door opened and there sat an old woman with a spindle, busily spinning flax.

"Good day, Granny," said the Princess. "What are you doing there?"

"I am spinning," answered the old woman, and nodded her head.

"What is the little thing that turns round so merrily?" asked the Princess, and she took the spindle and tried to spin, too. But the instant she touched it, the curse was fulfilled and she pricked her finger with the spindle.

A moment later, the Princess fell down upon a bed and lay quite still in a deep sleep. This sleep extended over the whole palace—the King and Queen, who had just returned home, and all the court, fell asleep, too. The horses slept in the stables, the dogs in the courtyard, the pigeons on the roofs and the flies on the walls. Even the fire on the hearth died down and went to sleep; and the meat stopped roasting, and the cook, who was at that moment pulling the kitchen-boy's hair for something he had done, let him go, and both fell asleep. And the wind was so quiet that not a leaf rustled on the trees around the castle.

Everything stood still, and everyone slept soundly.

A thick hedge of thorns soon grew around the castle, and every year it grew higher and higher, until at last it hid the whole palace from view. Not even the flag on the tower could be seen.

But the story of the beautiful sleeping Briar Rose (for that was the name of the Princess) went through the country, and from time to time several Princes came and tried to make their way through the thicket to the palace. They never succeeded, for the briars and thorns held them as if by hands, and the Princes were unable to free themselves.

After many, many years, a Prince came into the country from another land. He heard an old man tell the legend of the thicket of briars and thorns, and how a great castle stood behind it, in which slept a wonderfully beautiful Princess, and with her the King, the Queen and all their court.

He related, too, how a great number of Princes had tried to break through the thicket, but had been held fast.

Then the young Prince said, "All this does not frighten me. I will go and see this hedge of briars for myself!" The old man advised against it, but the Prince would not listen.

Now on that very day the hundred years were over, and as the Prince came to the thicket he saw nothing but flowering shrubs, through which he passed easily, and which closed behind him as firm as before. In the courtyard he saw the horses and dogs lying asleep, and on the roofs sat the pigeons with their heads under their wings; and when he came into the palace, he saw the flies sleeping on the walls, and the cook in the kitchen was still holding up her hand to strike the boy, and the maid sat with the fowl which she had been plucking still in her hand.

The Prince went on and saw the King and Queen asleep in the throne room, and he went on still farther, and all was so still that he could hear his own breathing, until at last he came to the old tower. He went up the steps to the door, opened it with the golden key, and saw the Princess lying asleep on the bed. She was so beautiful that he could not take his eyes from her, and he stooped and gave her a kiss. The moment he touched her, Briar Rose opened her eyes and smiled lovingly at him.

Then they went down out of the tower together, and the King and Queen awoke, and all the court awoke, too; and they gazed at each other in great wonder. The horses stood up and shook themselves, and the dogs ran about and barked; the pigeons lifted their heads from under their wings, looked around them and flew off over the fields; the flies on the walls buzzed away; the fire in the kitchen blazed up and cooked the dinner, and the roast meat turned round again. The cook gave the boy a slap so that he cried out, and the maid went on plucking the fowl.

Then the wedding of the Prince and Briar Rose was celebrated with pomp and splendor, and they lived happily together all the rest of their lives.

The Twelve Dancing Princesses

THERE was once a King who had twelve beautiful daughters. They slept all in one room, in twelve beds, and every night when they went to bed, the King locked the door and bolted it. Yet, in the morning, when he unlocked the door, he found his daughters' shoes worn to pieces, as if they had been danced in all night; and nobody could explain how it happened or where the Princesses went to dance.

So the King issued a proclamation, saying that anyone who could discover where the Princesses danced at night might have the one he liked best for his wife, and become King in his turn. But anyone who tried and failed to learn the secret, after three days and nights, would be put to death.

Soon afterward, a Prince came and offered to put himself to the task. He was well entertained, and in the evening was taken to a room next to the one where the twelve Princesses slept. There he was to watch and see where they went to dance. The door of his room was left open, so that he would be sure to miss nothing that might transpire. But the Prince soon fell asleep; and when he awoke next morning, he found that the Princesses had all been dancing in the night, for the soles of their shoes were full of holes. The same thing happened the second and third night, so the King ordered the Prince to be put to death. After him came many others who were willing to take the risk; but they all had the same luck, and all lost their lives in turn.

Now it happened that a poor soldier, who had been wounded in battle and could fight no longer, passed through the country where this King reigned. As he was traveling along the road, he met an old woman who asked him where he was going.

"I really don't know that myself," replied the soldier. "But I think I should like very much to find out where the Princesses dance, and then in time I would be a King."

"That is not too difficult," said the old woman. "Just be sure you do not drink any of the wine they will bring to you in the evening."

Then she gave him a cloak and said, "When you wear this, you will be invisible and you will be able to follow the Princesses wherever they go without being seen."

When the soldier heard all this good advice, he decided to try his luck, so he went before the King and told him he was willing to undertake the task.

He was well received, as the others had been, and the King ordered fine royal robes to be given him, and when it was time for bed, he was taken to the room next to the Princesses'. Just as he was lying down, the eldest of the Princesses brought him a cup of wine. But the soldier only pretended to drink it, and secretly threw it all away. Then he lay down on his bed, and in a little while began to snore loudly, as if he were fast asleep.

The Princesses, hearing this, shook their heads, and the youngest said sadly, "He is like all the others. He, too, will have to pay with his life."

Then they dressed themselves in all their fine clothes, and laughed and skipped before their looking glass, as if they could scarcely wait to begin dancing.

But the youngest said, "I don't know why it is, but while you are all so happy, I feel very uneasy. I am sure some misfortune will overtake us."

"You are a little goose," said the eldest. "You are always afraid. Have you forgotten how many Princes have already watched in vain? As for this soldier, even if I had not given him the sleeping draught, he would have slept soundly enough."

When they were all ready, they went in and looked at the soldier, but

he was still snoring and did not stir. So the Princesses felt quite safe, and the eldest went up to her own bed and clapped her hands. Instantly, the bed disappeared into the floor, and the Princesses descended into the opening, one after another, the eldest leading the way.

The soldier watched as the Princesses went down, then quickly put on the cloak the old woman had given him and followed them.

In the middle of the stairs, he stepped on the gown of the youngest Princess, who cried out, "Who is that? Who took hold of my dress?"

"Don't be silly," said the eldest. "You must have caught it on a nail."

Then down they all went, and at the bottom, far underground, they entered a delightful grove of trees. All the leaves were silver, and they shone and glittered beautifully.

"I must take some token of this place back with me," said the soldier to himself. So he broke off a little branch, and at the loud noise from the tree, the youngest said again, "Now I am sure all is not right! Surely you heard that cracking noise? That has never happened before."

"Nonsense!" said the eldest. "That is only our Princes, heralding our approach."

Next they came to another grove of trees, where all the leaves were of gold; and after that to a third grove, where all the leaves were glittering diamonds. At each grove, the soldier broke off a branch to take back with him, and each time there was a loud noise, so that the youngest Princess trembled with fear. But the eldest always told her it was the Princes, joyful at their coming. So they went on till they came to a great lake. At the side of the lake were twelve little boats, each with a handsome Prince in it. They had been waiting for the Princesses to arrive, and now each Prince took his Princess with him into his boat. The soldier stepped into the boat with the youngest and her Prince.

As they were rowing over the lake, the Prince who was in the boat with the youngest Princess and the soldier, said, "I don't know why, but the boat seems very heavy today. I am rowing with all my strength, but we scarcely seem to move, and I am already quite tired."

"It does seem so," said the youngest Princess. "Perhaps it is the weather. It is very warm today."

On the other side of the lake stood a great castle, brightly lighted, from which came the merry music of horns and trumpets. When they had landed, they all went into the castle, and each Prince danced with his Princess. The soldier, who had been invisible all this time, danced with them, too. And when one of the Princesses had a cup of wine, the soldier drank it, so that when she put the cup to her lips, she found it empty.

At this, the youngest Princess was more frightened than ever, but the eldest always silenced her.

They danced until three o'clock in the morning, when their shoes were worn to pieces, and they were obliged to stop.

The Princes rowed them back again over the lake, but this time the soldier got into the boat with the eldest Princess.

On the opposite shore, the Princesses said good-by to their Princes, promising to come again the next night.

When they reached the stairs, the soldier ran on ahead of the Princesses, and lay down in his bed, and as the Princesses came slowly, with dragging steps, into their bedroom, they heard him snoring. So they said, "We are quite safe," and undressed themselves and put away their beautiful clothes, put their worn-out shoes under their beds, and went to sleep.

In the morning, the soldier decided to say nothing about the strange adventure, for he wanted to see more the next night. So he went with the Princesses the second night and the third night, and everything happened exactly as on the first: the Princesses danced, as before, until their shoes were worn to shreds, and then returned home. On the third night, the soldier brought one of the golden cups back with him as a token.

When the time came for the soldier to go before the King with his report, he took the three branches and the golden cup with him. The twelve Princesses stood behind the door and listened to all that was said.

When the King asked him, "Where do my daughters dance at night?" the soldier answered, "With twelve Princes in a castle underground."

Then he told the King all that had happened, and gave him the three branches and the golden cup. The King called for the Princesses, and asked them whether the soldier spoke the truth. The Princesses realized that they were discovered, and that it was no use trying to deny what had happened, so they confessed everything.

The King thereupon asked the soldier which Princess he would choose for his wife, and the soldier answered, "Since I feel that I know her best of all, and that she knows me a little, I will take the youngest."

The King agreed, and they were married that very day, and the soldier was promised that he would be the next King.

Jorinda and Jorindel

IN an old castle that stood in the middle of a thick wood lived an old woman who was a witch. All day long she flew about in the form of an owl, or crept about like a cat. But at night she became an old woman again. When any man came within a hundred paces of her castle, he became motionless, as if turned to stone, and could not move a step till she came and set him free. But when a pretty maiden came within that distance, she was changed into a bird, and the witch put her into a cage which she hung in a room in the castle. There were seven hundred of these cages hanging in the castle, all with beautiful birds in them.

Now there was once a maiden named Jorinda, who was prettier than all the pretty girls who ever lived. She was loved by a handsome young man named Jorindel, and they were soon to be married.

One day, wishing to be alone together, they went for a walk in the wood. Jorindel said, "Be careful. We must not go too near the castle."

It was a beautiful evening. The last rays of the setting sun shone brightly through the trees onto the green undergrowth at their feet, and the turtledoves sang plaintively in the tall birch trees.

Jorinda sat down in the sunshine with Jorindel by her side. For some reason they could not explain, they both felt very sad, as if they were about to be parted from each other forever. By this time they had wandered a long way into the wood, and now, as they looked around them, they realized that they were lost and could not tell which path led to their homes.

The sun was sinking fast, and was already half-hidden behind the mountain. Jorindel looked through the bushes and saw, to his dismay, that they were sitting quite close to the old walls of the castle. He turned pale and trembled with fear. Jorinda was singing:

> *The ring-dove sings from the willow tree*
> *Sadly, oh! sadly—*
> *He mourns the fate*
> *Of his pretty mate—*
> *Sadly, so sadly!*

The song ceased abruptly. Jorindel turned to look at Jorinda and found her changed into a nightingale, and her song ended with a mournful note. An owl with fiery eyes flew three times around them, and three times screamed, "Whoo! Whoo! Whoo!" Jorindel could not move. He stood as if turned to stone, and could not speak or cry out, or stir hand or foot. And now the sun was gone completely, and in the gloom the owl flew into a bush, and a moment later the old woman came out of it. She was skinny and yellow with fiery red eyes and a nose so long and crooked that it almost touched her chin. Mumbling to herself, she caught the nightingale and went away with it in her hand. Jorindel could do nothing but watch them go, for he could not speak or move from the spot where he stood.

At last the old woman came back and said in a droning voice:

> The prisoner's fast,
> And her doom is cast,
> So away! away!
> The charm is around her,
> The spell has bound her.
> Go away! away!

Suddenly, Jorindel found that he was free. He fell on his knees before the old woman and begged her to give his dear Jorinda back to him. But she said he would never see her again, and went away. Jorindel pleaded, he prayed, he wept, but all in vain. "Alas!" he cried. "What is to become of me now?"

He could not return to his own home, so he went to a strange village, where he found work as a shepherd. He spent his free time wandering around the hated castle, going as close to it as he dared. At last he dreamed one night that he found a beautiful purple flower, in the middle of which lay a costly pearl. He dreamed that he plucked the flower and took it into the castle, and everything he touched with it became disenchanted, and in this way he found his Jorinda again.

In the morning, when he awoke, he began to search over hill and dale for a flower like the one he had seen in his dream. He searched for eight days without success, but early in the morning of the ninth day he found the purple flower; and in the middle of it was a large dewdrop as big as the pearl had been.

Jorindel took the flower and carried it with him day and night until he reached the castle. He walked nearer than the hundred paces, and found that he was not held fast, as before. He went right up to the door.

Overjoyed, Jorindel touched the door with the flower and it sprang open, and he went in through the courtyard. As he walked, he could hear the sound of many birds singing.

Then he came into the room where the old witch sat with the seven hundred birds in seven hundred cages around her. When she saw Jorindel, she turned black with rage, spitting and screaming at him. But she could not come within two yards of him, for the flower he held in his hand protected him from her sorcery.

Jorindel looked around at the birds, but alas! there were so many, many nightingales! How could he tell which one was Jorinda?

While he was looking and thinking what to do, he noticed that the old woman had taken down one of the cages with a bird inside, and was creeping stealthily toward the door. He sprang after her and touched the witch and the bird with the flower. The witch lost her power completely —and Jorinda stood before him, as beautiful as ever! She threw her arms around Jorindel's neck and wept for joy.

Then Jorindel touched all the other birds with the flower, so that they all became maidens again; and he took his dear Jorinda home. They were married soon after, and lived happily together for many, many years.

The Giant With the Three Golden Hairs

THERE was once a poor man who had only one son. The child had been born under a lucky star, and it was foretold of him that in his eighteenth year he would marry the King's daughter.

Soon after this, it happened that the King passed through the village in disguise, and when he asked the people what news there was, they answered, "A child has just been born and they say he is fated to marry the King's daughter when he is eighteen years old."

The King was greatly disturbed by this prophecy. He went to the child's parents and said, "Let me take the boy. I'll bring him up properly and care for him."

They refused. However, when the stranger offered them a great deal of money, they at last consented, for they were very poor. "Besides," they said to themselves, "he is a luck-child and no harm can come to him."

The King put the boy in a box and rode away; and when he came to a stream that was very deep, he threw the box into the current, thinking, "That's one prophecy that will never be fulfilled!"

The box, however, did not sink. It floated down the stream like a little boat and did not even leak; the child remained dry and safe inside. At last, it stopped at the dam of a mill two miles from the King's palace. The miller saw it and drew it to the shore with a long pole, thinking he had found a treasure. But when he opened the box, he found a beautiful child who smiled merrily up at him.

Now the miller and his wife had no children, and they were over-joyed. "Heaven has sent him to us," they said, and they cared for him as if he had been their own child, so that he grew into a fine, handsome lad admired by everyone.

Years went by, and then one day the King was passing the mill when a sudden storm caused him to find shelter there. He saw the tall young man and asked the miller if this was his son.

"No," replied the miller, "I found him in a box in the mill-dam when he was a tiny babe—almost eighteen years ago."

"He is a fine boy," said the King. "Can you spare him for a short while so that he might carry a letter to my wife the Queen? I'll give him two pieces of gold for his trouble."

"As your majesty commands," said the miller, and told his son to prepare for the journey.

Now the King had realized that the boy was none other than the luck-child he had tried to drown in the stream, so he wrote to the Queen, saying, "As soon as the bearer of this arrives, let him be killed and buried at once, so that all will be over when I return."

The young man set out on his journey with the letter, but he lost his way, and when evening came he found himself in a great forest. Through the darkness he saw a small light, and going toward it he found that it came from a small cottage. He went in and there was an old woman sitting by the fire.

Upon seeing the young man, the old woman was filled with terror, and cried, "What are you doing here? Where are you going?"

"I'm on my way to the Queen, to whom I must deliver a letter," he told her. "But I've lost my way in this dark wood and I shall be very grateful if I may stay here until morning."

"You can't stay here," she said. "This is a robbers' hut. If they find you when they return, they'll murder you!"

"I'll take my chances," he replied, "for I'm too tired to go a step farther." And he settled himself on a bench and went to sleep.

A short time later, the robbers came home and demanded to know who the strange lad was.

"He's just a poor innocent who lost his way in the wood," the old woman said. "I pitied him, so I let him stay the night. He is carrying a letter to the Queen."

The robbers took the letter and opened it. When they read it and realized that it contained the boy's death sentence, they took pity on him, too, and they tore the letter up and wrote another. The second letter said that the young man was to marry the King's daughter the moment he arrived at the palace.

They let the lad sleep until morning, and when he awoke they showed him the right path to the palace, and sent him on his way with the letter in his pocket.

As soon as the Queen received the letter, she did as it commanded and made all the arrangements for the wedding. Since the young man was very handsome, the Princess loved him at first sight, and was delighted to be his bride.

And when the King returned to the palace soon afterward, he found that the prophecy had been fulfilled.

"How did this happen?" he demanded. "My letter contained a different command!"

The Queen gave him the letter and the King read for himself what was written in it. He realized that it had been changed for the one he himself had written, and asked the young man what had become of the letter he had entrusted to him.

"I don't know," he replied. "It must have been exchanged in the forest where I spent the night."

Then the King turned white with rage and cried, "No man shall have my daughter unless he descends into the great cave and brings me three golden hairs from the head of the giant who lives there! Do this and I'll give my consent."

"I'm sure I can manage that," said the young man. He said good-by to the Princess and hurried off to find the great cave and the giant.

At the first town he came to, the guard at the gate stopped him and asked him his trade and what he knew. "I know everything," replied the young man.

"In that case, you're just the person we've been waiting for. Be so good as to tell us why the fountain in the market place will give no more water."

"I'll tell you gladly," he replied, "when I come back."

Then he went on and came to another town, and there the guard also asked him his trade and what he understood. "I understand everything," the young man answered.

"Then help us, please," said the guard. "Tell us why a tree growing in the park, which once bore golden apples, now does not even produce a leaf."

"Most willingly," he answered, "when I come back."

He went on, and at last his path led him to the side of a great lake over which he must travel. The ferryman soon asked him what his trade was and what he knew.

"I know everything," he said.

"Then you can do me a great favor," said the ferryman. "Tell me why

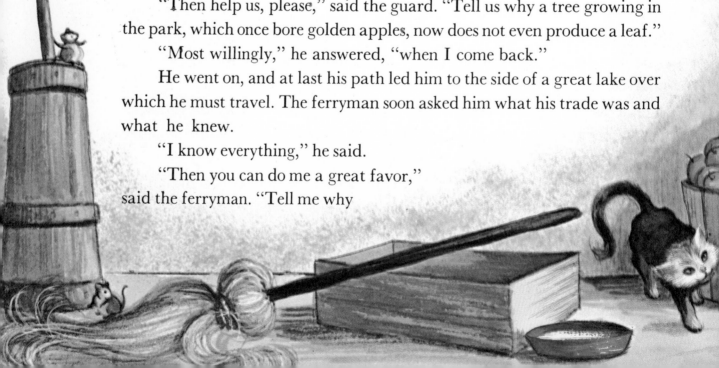

I must row back and forth over this lake and can never stop."

"I'll tell you that," said the young man, "when I come home."

Then they reached the other side of the lake, and the young man found himself at the entrance of the giant's dark cave. The giant was not at home, but his grandmother sat at the door in her easy chair.

"What do you want?" she asked, staring at him.

"Three golden hairs from the giant's head," he answered.

"You ask for a great deal," she said. "If he finds you here when he returns, it will be bad for you. However, stay and I'll see if I can help you."

"Good," he said, "but I also need to know why the fountain is dry, why the tree that bore golden apples is now leafless, and what it is that binds the ferryman to his boat."

"What difficult questions!" said the old woman. Then she changed him into an ant and hid him in the folds of her dress.

"Now lie quietly and listen to all the giant says when I pull the golden hairs from his head," she said.

In a little while, the giant came home. As soon as he entered the cave, he sniffed the air and cried, "All is not right here! I smell the flesh of a man!"

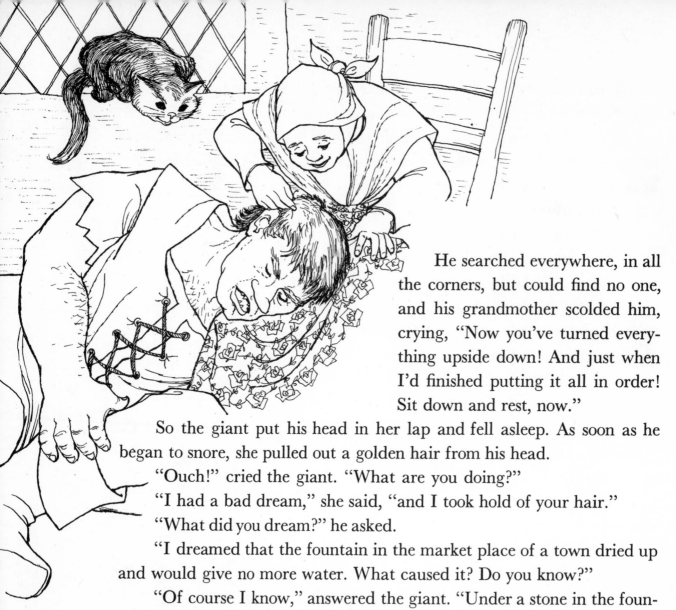

He searched everywhere, in all the corners, but could find no one, and his grandmother scolded him, crying, "Now you've turned everything upside down! And just when I'd finished putting it all in order! Sit down and rest, now."

So the giant put his head in her lap and fell asleep. As soon as he began to snore, she pulled out a golden hair from his head.

"Ouch!" cried the giant. "What are you doing?"

"I had a bad dream," she said, "and I took hold of your hair."

"What did you dream?" he asked.

"I dreamed that the fountain in the market place of a town dried up and would give no more water. What caused it? Do you know?"

"Of course I know," answered the giant. "Under a stone in the fountain sits a toad. When they get rid of him, the fountain will flow again."

Having said this, he fell asleep once more, and the old woman pulled out another golden hair.

"Now what are you doing?" cried the giant in a rage.

"Don't be cross," she said. "I did it in my sleep. I was dreaming again."

"And what did you dream this time?" he asked.

"I dreamed that in a great kingdom there grows a beautiful tree which once bore golden apples, but which now does not even have a single leaf. What is the reason for that?"

"Aha!" said the giant. "That is a secret they would like to know. At the root of the tree a mouse is gnawing. If they get rid of him, the tree will bear golden apples again. Otherwise, the tree will soon die altogether. Now let me sleep in peace. If you wake me again, you'll regret it!"

28

So the old woman rocked him to sleep again, and when he was snoring, she pulled out the third golden hair. The giant jumped up, roaring at her in a terrible fury, but she soothed him and said, "This was the strangest dream of all. I thought I saw a ferryman who was doomed to row back and forth across a lake, and could never stop. What is the charm that binds him?"

"He's a silly fool!" said the giant. "If he were to give the oar to one of his passengers, he would find himself free and the other would have to row in his place. Now let me sleep."

Next morning, after the giant left the cave, the woman returned the young man to his proper form again and put the three golden hairs into his hand. Then she reminded him of the answers to his three questions and sent him on his way.

When he came to the lake, the ferryman asked for the answer that he had promised to bring to him. "Row me across first and then I will tell you how you may be freed," he answered. And when the boat reached the other side, he told the man that all he had to do was give the oar to his next passenger and he would be able to go, a free man.

Then he went on to the city where the barren tree stood in the market place. "Get rid of the mouse gnawing at the root of the tree, and it will bear golden apples again," he said. They gave him two donkeys laden with gold, and he went on to the town where the dry fountain was. He told the guard how to cure the trouble, and they thanked him and gave him two more donkeys laden with gold. And now at last the lucky young man reached home, where he was greeted with great joy by his wife. He gave the three golden hairs to the King, and when the King saw the four donkeys laden with gold, he was delighted.

"You have fulfilled all the conditions, and so you may now have my daughter in marriage," he said. "But where did you find all this gold?"

"By the side of a lake," replied the young man.

"Can I get some of it, do you suppose?" asked the King.

"Certainly," said the other. "Let the ferryman row you across the lake and there you will see the gold lying on the shore like sand."

Away went the greedy King; and when he came to the lake, he beckoned to the ferryman, who took him into his boat. When they reached the other side, the ferryman put the oar into the King's hand and sprang ashore. So the King was left to row back and forth in his place.

No doubt he is still rowing to this day, since nobody will trouble to take the oar out of his hands.

Maid Maleen

ONCE, long ago, there lived a Prince who wished to marry the daughter of the mighty King of a neighboring country. She was called Maid Maleen and she was very lovely. Her father planned to marry her to another, so the Prince was rejected. But they loved each other deeply, and refused to be parted.

"If I cannot marry my Prince," Maid Maleen said to her father, "I shall marry no one."

Then the King flew into a passion, and he ordered a tower to be built near the castle, into which no ray from the sun or moon should enter. When it was finished, he said, "This shall be your prison for seven years. By that time, your stubborn spirit will be broken and you will obey me."

Food and drink enough for seven years were placed inside the tower, and then the Princess and her waiting-maid were taken into it, the last opening was walled up, and they were shut away from the sky and the earth. There they sat in darkness, never knowing when day ended or night began. The unhappy Prince went round and round the tower, many times, called, "Maleen! Maid Maleen!" but neither his voice nor any other sound could penetrate the thick walls.

31

Time passed, and by the diminishing store of food and water, they knew that the seven years were almost over. They began to listen for the sound of the hammer that would free them, and for the first stones to fall from the wall, but no sound came.

"Alas, my father has forgotten us!" said Maid Maleen. "We must try to break through the wall. It is our only chance, for we have food for only a few days more."

She took the bread-knife and picked and dug at the mortar between the stones, and when she grew tired, the waiting-maid took her turn. They finally succeeded in getting out one stone, and then a second and a third, and three days later the first ray of light invaded the darkness of the tower. Then, at last, the opening was large enough for them to look out. They saw a blue sky above, and a fresh breeze played gently over their faces. But everything around them, as far as they could see, lay in ruins. Her father's castle, the towns and villages were gone, destroyed by what must have been a great fire, and the fields far and wide were a desolate wasteland. No human being was to be seen anywhere.

When the opening in the wall was large enough for them to slip through, the waiting-maid climbed out first and then Maid Maleen followed. But where were they to go? The enemy had ravaged the entire kingdom. The King and all the inhabitants had fled or been killed.

They wandered over the countryside, looking for food and a place to stay, but they could find none, and were forced to eat nettles to keep from starving. At last, after they had wandered a long time, they came to another country, where they tried to find work in order to earn enough to eat. But they were turned away from every door. No one, it seemed, would have pity on them. Then they reached a large city, and went to the royal palace. There, too, they were turned away, but the cook, who needed help, said that they might stay and work as kitchen-maids.

Now it happened that the castle in which they had found refuge was that of the King to whose son Maid Maleen had been betrothed. The King had chosen another bride for his son, but she was as ugly and wicked as Maleen was beautiful and good. The wedding of the Prince to this maiden had been announced, and she was already in the castle, preparing for the wedding. But since she did not want anyone to see how ugly she was, she shut herself up in her room, admitting no one except Maid Maleen, who had to take her meals to her from the kitchen.

When the day of the wedding arrived, the bride was afraid to show herself, fearing that she would be mocked and laughed at by the people. She looked at beautiful Maid Maleen and said, "You are in luck! I've sprained my ankle and won't be able to walk to the church. You must put on my wedding gown and take my place. Think what a great honor it will be for you!"

But Maid Maleen refused to do as she asked, and said, "I do not want such an honor. It is not suitable for me."

The bride offered her gold. Still Maid Maleen refused. At last, the bride cried angrily, "Obey me or I shall have you killed."

So Maid Maleen was forced to obey, and she put on the bride's splendid robes and all her jewels. When she entered the great hall, everyone gasped to see her great beauty.

The bridegroom was speechless with astonishment. "She is so like my dear Maid Maleen, that I would think it was she standing there if I did not know she is shut up in the tower, and probably dead," he thought.

He took her by the hand and led her to the church. On the way, they passed a stinging nettle, and she said:

"Nettle, nettle, growing alone,
A time of sorrow I have known—
Nothing to eat was there for me.
Hunger forced me to eat thee."

"What are you saying?" asked the Prince.

"Nothing," she answered. "I was only thinking of Maid Maleen."

The Prince wondered how she knew about Maid Maleen, but he said nothing more. When they came to the stile in the churchyard, she said:

"Church stile, hold fast,
The true bride will come at last."

"What are you saying now?" asked the Prince.

"Nothing," she replied. "I was only thinking of Maid Maleen."

"Do you know Maid Maleen, then?"

"No," she answered. "How could I? I have only heard of her."

When they came to the church door, she said:

"Church door, do not break,
Do not break for the true bride's sake."

"Now what are you saying?" asked the Prince.

"Ah," she answered, "I was only thinking of Maid Maleen."

34

Then the Prince put a beautiful jewel on a chain around her neck and fastened the clasp. They entered the church and were married.

When they returned to the royal palace, Maid Maleen hurried to the bride's room and took off the royal robes and jewels, and dressed herself in her old clothes again, keeping nothing but the jewel on her neck that the Prince had given her.

Night came, and the bride, her face heavily veiled so that it could not be seen, was led to the Prince's room. As soon as they were alone, he said to her, "What did you say to the stinging nettle growing by the wayside?"

"What stinging nettle?" asked the bride. "I do not talk to nettles."

"If you did not, you are not the true bride," he said.

The bride thought a moment and then said, "I must go and see my maid, who keeps my thoughts for me."

She went out and found Maid Maleen in the kitchen.

"Girl," she said, "what have you been saying to the nettle?"

Maid Maleen answered, "I only said:

"Nettle, nettle, growing alone,
A time of sorrow I have known—
Nothing to eat was there for me.
Hunger forced me to eat thee."

The bride hurried back to the Prince and said, "I remember what I said to the nettle." And she repeated the words she had just been told.

"But what did you say to the stile when we went over it?" asked the Prince.

"To the stile? I don't talk to stiles!" she answered.

"Then you are not the true bride!"

She said quickly, "I must go and find my maid who keeps my thoughts for me." And she hurried out to find Maid Maleen again. "Girl, what did you say to the stile?" she demanded.

"I said:

> "Church stile, hold fast,
> The true bride will come at last."

"You shall die for this!" cried the false bride, but she hurried back into the room and repeated Maid Maleen's words to the Prince.

"And what did you say to the church door?" he asked.

"To the church door? I do not talk to church doors!" she replied.

"Then you are not the true bride!"

She went out again and found Maid Maleen. "Girl," she cried angrily, "what did you say to the church door?"

Maid Maleen answered, "I said:

> "Church door, do not break,
> Do not break for the true bride's sake."

"You shall pay for this!" the bride cried, very angry by now. Then she hurried back to the Prince and said, "I remember now what I said to the church door," and she repeated the words.

"But where is the jewel I gave you at the church door?" asked the Prince.

"What jewel?" she cried. "You did not give me a jewel."

"I put it around your neck myself, and fastened it. If you do not know that, you are not the true bride."

And he drew the veil from her face. When he saw how ugly she was, he sprang back in alarm. "Who are you? How did you get here?" he cried.

"I am your bride," she told him. "But I was afraid the people would mock me when they saw my face, so I commanded the scullery-maid to dress herself in my robes and take my place beside you at the church."

"Where is this girl?" demanded the Prince. "I wish to see her. Go and bring her here!"

The bride went out, but she told the servants that the scullery-maid was an imposter, and ordered them to take her into the courtyard and do away with her. The servants caught Maid Maleen and tried to drag her away, but she screamed so loudly for help that the Prince heard her and came running.

He ordered the servants to let her go at once. Then, holding a light up to her, he saw her beautiful face and on her neck the gold chain he had given to her at the church door.

"You are my true bride," he said. "You went with me to the church. Come with me now."

When they were alone, he said, "You mentioned Maid Maleen on the way to the church. She was my betrothed bride, long ago. If such a thing could be, I would think she was standing before me now. You are like her in every way."

She answered, "I am Maid Maleen, who was imprisoned for seven years in the dark tower for your sake. I have suffered hunger and thirst, and lived in great poverty. But now the sun is shining for me again. I was married to you in the church today and I am your lawful wife." Then they kissed each other long and joyfully, and spent the rest of their lives together in great happiness. The false bride was banished from the country, and was never allowed to return.

The dark tower in which Maid Maleen had been imprisoned remained standing for a long time, and when the children passed by they sang:

"Sunshine and shower—
Who sits in the tower?
A King's daughter sits inside.
I cannot save her, though I've tried.
The wall, it will not break,
The stone, it will not crack.
Little one, with your smile so gay,
Follow me, follow me, fast as you may."

The Goose Girl

AN OLD Queen, whose husband had been dead for many years, had a
beautiful daughter. The daughter was betrothed to a Prince in a
far-off country, and as the time drew near for her to go to him, the
old Queen packed up quantities of fine clothes and many jewels, gold and
silver, ornaments, cups and trinkets of all kinds—in fact, everything suitable for a royal bride, for she loved her daughter dearly.

She also gave her a waiting-maid to ride with her and put her safely
into the Prince's hands. They each had a horse for the journey. The Princess's horse was named Falada, and it could speak.

When it was time for her daughter to depart, the Queen went into
her bedroom and cut off a lock of her hair, which she gave to her daughter.
"Take good care of it, my child," she said. "It is a charm, and may be of
use to you on the journey."

They said good-by tearfully, and the Princess put the lock of her
mother's hair into her bosom. Then she mounted Falada and, with the
waiting-maid following close behind on the other horse, she set out on the
journey to the bridegroom's kingdom.

After they had been riding for a time, the Princess became thirsty,
and when they came to a brook, she said to her waiting-maid, "I must
have a drink. Do get down and bring me some water in my golden cup."

"Get down yourself and drink from the brook, if you're thirsty,"
replied the waiting-maid. "I won't be your servant any longer!"

The Princess was so thirsty that she got down and knelt at the little
brook and drank, not daring to ask for her golden cup.

"Alas!" she said, and the lock of her mother's hair answered:
> *"Yes, alas!*
>> *If your mother knew your fate,*
>> *Surely her poor heart would break."*

The Princess, who was meek and gentle, said nothing to her waiting-maid, but mounted her horse once more. They rode on, and the day grew warmer and warmer, the sun so scorching, that the Princess began to feel very thirsty again. When they came to a river, she forgot the waiting-maid's rudeness and said, "Do get down and bring me some water."

But the maid answered even more haughtily than before, "Get down yourself and drink, if you must. I am not your servant."

Being too thirsty to resist, the Princess dismounted and leaned over the flowing water. "Alas!" she said to herself, weeping. "What will become of me?"

And the lock of hair answered:
> *"Yes, alas!*
>> *If your mother knew your fate,*
>> *Surely her poor heart would break."*

Now, as the Princess leaned over the water to drink, the lock of hair fell from her dress and floated away on the water. The Princess, whose eyes were full of tears, did not notice, but the waiting-maid saw it and was elated, for she knew of the charm, and realized that without the lock of hair the Princess was in her power.

And when the Princess was about to mount Falada again, the maid cried, "No! I shall ride Falada. You shall take my old horse instead."

She forced the Princess to change horses with her, and ordered her to take off her royal robes and put on the maid's shabby garments. Finally, the Princess had to swear before heaven never to reveal to anyone what had happened, or the waiting-maid would have killed her on the spot. But Falada saw it all and marked it well.

Then the waiting-maid mounted Falada and the Princess took the other horse, and they continued on the journey.

There was great joy in the court when they arrived, and the Prince ran to meet them. He lifted the waiting-maid from Falada, thinking she was his bride-to-be, and led her up the steps to her royal apartments, while the true Princess had to remain in the courtyard.

The old King looked out of the window and saw the pretty, delicate creature standing alone in the courtyard. So he went to the royal apartments and asked the bride-to-be who it was she had left standing below in the courtyard.

"I brought her with me for company on the road," she replied. "Give her something to do so that she will not be idle."

The old King could not think of any work fit for such a delicate girl, but at last he said, "I have a lad who

takes care of my geese. She may go and help him."

So the real Princess was sent to help the lad, whose name was Curd-ken, take care of his geese.

Soon after this, the waiting-maid said to the Prince, "Dear one, I have a favor to ask of you."

"Certainly," said the Prince. "What is it?"

"Tell one of your men to cut off the head of the horse I rode when I came. It is an unruly beast and angered me all the way."

The truth was, however, that she was afraid Falada might speak, and tell what she had done to the Princess. Falada was led away to be killed; but the true Princess saw it and wept, and begged the man not to kill Falada, but to give the horse to her. She would care for it and see that it bothered no one.

The man shrugged and gave the horse to her, glad to be rid of a distasteful job. The Princess hid Falada in a nearby stable.

Next morning, as the Princess and Curdken were passing the stable, the Princess said sadly:

> *"Alas, Falada, what will become of us?"*

And Falada answered:

> *"Princess, alas, indeed!*
> *If your mother knew your fate,*
> *Surely her poor heart would break."*

Then they drove the geese along before them out of the city. When they reached the meadow, the Princess sat down on a rock and let her beautiful hair fall down over her shoulders. It was like pure gold in the sunlight. Curdken was so charmed by its glittering brightness that he tried to pull out a lock of it. So she sang:

> *"Blow, breezes, blow!*
> *Let Curdken's hat go.*
> *Blow, breezes, blow—*
> *Make him after it go.*
> *Over hill and dale and rocks,*
> *Away let it be whirled,*
> *Till my golden locks*
> *Are all combed and curled!"*

Suddenly, a strong wind blew Curdken's hat off and carried it over the hills, and he had to run after it. By the time he returned, she had finished combing and curling her hair, and had put it up again. Then, together, they watched the geese until evening came.

The next day, the same thing happened, and when they went home Curdken hurried to the King and said, "I don't want that strange girl to help me tend the geese any longer."

"Why not?" asked the King.

"Because she teases me all day long!"

The old King ordered Curdken to tell him how she teased him so, and Curdken said, "Every morning, as we pass a stable on our way to the meadow, she talks to a horse inside, and says, 'Alas, Falada, what will become of us?' And the horse answers:

> *'Princess, alas, indeed!*
> *If your mother knew your fate,*
> *Surely her poor heart would break.' "*

Then Curdken went on and told the King all that had happened in the meadow—how the goose girl took down her hair to comb it, and how the wind blew his hat off so that he had to run after it.

The old King told Curdken to go out again as usual next morning; and when morning came, the King placed himself behind the stable door and heard how she spoke to Falada. Then he followed them into the meadow, and hid behind a bush. He saw with his own eyes how the goose girl let down her hair and how it glittered like gold in the sun. He watched as Curdken tried to pull some of it out, and he heard the girl sing:

> *"Blow, breezes, blow!*
> *Let Curdken's hat go.*
> *Blow, breezes, blow!*
> *Make him after it go.*
> *Over hill and dale and rocks,*
> *Away let it be whirled,*
> *Till my golden locks*
> *Are all combed and curled!"*

Then a puff of wind carried Curdken's hat far away over the hills and he had to run after it. While he was gone, the goose girl combed and curled her hair and put it up again. The King saw it all, and went away without being noticed. In the evening, the King called the goose girl to him and asked her why she did these things.

"I may not tell you that," she answered, "for I've sworn before heaven never to tell anyone." And she burst into tears.

The King insisted on knowing everything, but she would not reveal anything. Then he said, "Tell your sorrows to the iron stove there, if not to me!" And he went out. The Princess crept to the stove, still weeping, and relieved her heart by talking to it. "Here I am," she said, "forsaken by everyone, and yet I am a Princess. A false waiting-maid compelled me to change places with her, and she is in the palace about to marry the Prince, while I am only a common goose girl. Oh! If my mother knew my fate, surely her poor heart would break!"

The old King, meanwhile, stood outside and heard all that she said. Then he ordered royal robes for her, and when she was dressed in them, she was so beautiful that he gazed at her in wonder. He called his son and told him he was about to be married to a waiting-maid, not the true Princess, who stood there before them.

The Prince was charmed with her great beauty and her youth. A great feast was prepared, to which all the court was invited. The Prince sat at the head of the table, with the waiting-maid on one side and the Princess on the other. But the waiting-maid did not recognize the Princess in her dazzling costume.

When they had eaten and drunk and were very merry, the King told the story of the Princess and the waiting-maid. When he had finished, he turned to the waiting-maid and said; "What would you do to anyone who behaved in this way?"

The waiting-maid answered, "She should be thrown into a cask and dragged through the streets."

"That shall be your fate, then, since you are the guilty one!" cried the King.

But the Princess begged the King to spare the waiting-maid and not send her to such a horrible death, however much she deserved it.

"What would you do with her?" asked the Prince.

"Send her into a far-off country, and let her wander there, homeless and penniless, until she learns to love her fellow creatures and treat them kindly."

The old King said, "Let it be so," and the waiting-maid was taken away.

The Prince married the true Princess and they reigned in peace and joy all their lives. Falada was allowed to roam free in the pasture around the castle, a royal horse. But he never spoke again.

The Peasant's Wise Daughter

THERE was once a poor peasant who had no land, but only a small cottage and one daughter.

"Perhaps the King will give us a bit of the land that has just been cleared, if we ask him," said the daughter one day.

When the King heard how poor they were, he presented them with a little field, and the man and his daughter began at once to plow the field, intending to plant corn and other grains in it. They had turned over all but a small portion of the field when they unearthed a mortar of pure gold.

"We must take it to the King," said the father. "Since he has been so kind to us, we can thank him in this way."

The daughter, however, shook her head. "If we take the mortar to the King," she reasoned, "he will want the pestle too, for what good is it to have a mortar to grind grains and herbs in, if one doesn't have the pestle to grind them with? Since we don't have the pestle, we had better say nothing at all about it."

But her father would not listen. He took the golden mortar to the King, told him he had found it in the cleared land, and begged him to accept it as a token of their gratitude.

The King accepted the mortar, but said, "What else did you find in the field?"

"Nothing else," replied the peasant.

The King refused to believe this and told him to go and bring the

pestle. The peasant tried to
explain that they had found
no pestle, but he might as well
have spoken to the wind. He
was put in prison, and told he
would have to stay there until
he produced the pestle.

Later, when the servants
took food and water to the
prison, they heard the peasant
cry out over and over, "Ah!
If only I had listened to my
daughter! If only I had listened to my daughter!"

They hurried to the King and told him what the man had cried out
over and over, and how he refused to eat or drink. The King ordered the
prisoner brought before him, and asked him why he kept crying, "Ah, if
only I had listened to my daughter!" and what it was his daughter had said.

"She told me that I must not take the mortar to you, for I should
have to produce the pestle as well."

"If you have a daughter as wise as that, send her to me," said the
King. So the daughter had to go before the King, who said to her, "If you
are really so wise, I will give you a riddle to solve. If you can solve it, you
shall be my Queen." The daughter agreed.

The King said, "Come to me not clothed, not naked, not riding, not
walking, not in the road, and not out of the road, and if you can do this,
you shall be my Queen."

The daughter left. She took off everything she had on, and then she
was not clothed; and next she took a great fishing-net, seated herself in the
middle of it, and wound it round and round her, and then she was not
naked; then she hired an old donkey, tied the fisherman's net to it so that
it had to drag her along, and so she was neither riding nor walking. The
donkey had to drag her along in the cart-ruts, so that only one of her toes
touched the ground, and so she was neither in the road nor out of the road.

48

In this fashion, she arrived at the palace, and when the King saw her he said that she had guessed the riddle and fulfilled all the conditions. He ordered her father released from prison, took the daughter to be his Queen, and gave all the royal possessions into her care.

Several years passed. One day, the King was reviewing his troops on parade, when some farmers who had been selling wood stopped their wagons in front of the palace. Some of the wagons were drawn by oxen, some by horses, and one of the farmers had three horses hitched to his wagon. One of the horses had a foal, and it ran over and lay down between the two oxen that were yoked to the wagon in front. The farmers immediately began to argue, and soon came to blows, because the farmer with the oxen wanted to keep the foal, insisting that it belonged to one of his oxen, while the other farmer said it belonged to his mare and that it was his.

The dispute was laid before the King, who said that the foal should stay where it had been found. So the farmer with the oxen, to whom the foal did not belong, took it away with him. The other farmer went away, too, weeping and lamenting the loss of his foal. Now, he had heard that the Queen had been a poor country girl before her marriage to the King, and knowing how kind and gracious she was, he went to her and begged her to help him recover his foal.

"Yes, I think I can help you," said the Queen, "if you will do exactly as I tell you, and promise never to let anyone know who advised you."

The farmer promised, and she continued, "Early tomorrow morning, when the King parades the guards, place yourself in the middle of the road by which he must pass. Take a fishing-net and pretend to be fishing. Go on fishing, and empty out the net as if it were full of fish." Then she told him what to say if the King questioned him.

The next morning, the farmer did as the Queen had directed, and fished on dry ground. When the King passed by and saw this, he sent one of his guardsmen to ask what the foolish man was doing.

The farmer answered, "I am fishing."

"How can you fish where there is no water?" asked the guardsman.

The farmer answered, "It is just as easy for me to fish on dry land as it is for an ox to have a foal."

The guardsman went back to the King and told him this, and the King ordered the farmer to be brought to him. The King said, "You are right—and I shall see that you get your foal back again. But this can't have been your idea. Who told you to do it?"

The farmer insisted that it was his own idea, but they beat him until at last he admitted that the Queen had advised him what to do.

The King went back to the palace and said to the Queen, "Why did you behave so falsely to me? You are no longer my wife! Go back where you came from—to your peasant's hut!"

One favor, however, he granted her: she might take with her the one thing that was dearest and best in her eyes. And so she was dismissed.

The Queen threw her arms around him and kissed him. "Yes, dear husband," she said, "if you command me to go, I'll go. But first, let us drink a little wine in farewell."

When the wine was brought, she slipped a strong sleeping draught into it. The King drank all of his at once, but she drank only a very little from her own glass.

The King soon fell into a deep sleep, and when she saw that he was asleep, she called a servant, and together they wrapped the King in a white linen sheet. Then the servant put the King into a carriage waiting at the door and she drove home with him to her father's cottage.

She laid him in her own little bed, where he slept one whole day and a night without waking. When he finally opened his eyes, he looked around him and cried, "Bless me! Where am I?" He called his attendants, but none were there.

Instead, his wife came and stood by his bed, and said, "My Lord and King, you told me to take with me whatever was dearest and most precious in my eyes. I have nothing more precious than you yourself, so I brought you with me."

Tears came to the King's eyes, and he said, "Dear wife, you are mine and I am yours." And he took her back with him to the palace, where they lived in perfect peace and happiness the rest of their lives.

The Golden Goose

THERE was once a man who had three sons. The youngest was called Dummling, and was scorned and ill-treated by the whole family.

One day, the eldest son went into the forest to cut wood. His mother gave him a delicious sweet cake and a jug of milk to take with him so that he might refresh himself during the day.

As he walked along the path, a little old man stopped him.

"Good morning," he said. "I am so hungry and thirsty! Give me a bit of your cake and a drop of the milk you carry in your pocket."

But this clever son said, "If I did that, I would not have enough for myself. Out of my way!" And he went on, leaving the little old man standing there.

Soon after, he began to cut down a tree, but after a few blows from his ax, he missed the tree and struck his own arm, so that he was obliged to run home and have it bandaged.

Now, this had been no accident. The little old man had caused it to happen.

The second son now went into the forest to cut wood, and his mother gave him a sweet cake and a jug of milk, also. And the same little man met him and asked for something to eat and drink. The second son was as clever as the first, and said, "If I give some to you, I will have less for myself. So be off!"

The little old man saw to it that the second brother received his reward for this kindness. At the second stroke, he aimed at the tree, he struck his leg and was forced to limp home.

Then Dummling said, "Father, let me go out and cut the wood."

But his father said, "Both your brothers have hurt themselves. You'd better stay at home, since you know nothing about wood-cutting."

But Dummling begged so hard to be allowed to go that at last his father said, "Well, go on, then. You will come home a wiser lad, at least."

His mother gave him a piece of dry bread and a jug of water to take with him, and he started off. He, too, met the little old man who said, "Give me a bit of your food and milk. I'm so hungry and thirsty."

Dummling replied, "I have only dry bread and water, but you're welcome to share that with me, if you like."

They sat down to eat, but when Dummling brought out the bread, it had turned into a golden, sweet cake, and the water had become fresh milk. Then they ate and drank heartily, and the old man said, "As you have such a kind heart and shared your bit of food with me, I will put a blessing upon you. There stands an old tree. Cut it down and you will find something at the roots."

Dummling cut down the tree, and when it fell, a goose was sitting at the roots, and its feathers were pure gold. He picked it up and walked to a nearby inn, where he planned to spend the night.

The landlord had three daughters, and when they saw the goose, they were curious as to what kind of bird it was. They longed to have one of its golden feathers.

The eldest thought, "I'll get a feather, somehow." She waited until Dummling's back was turned, then she seized the goose by the wing. To her great surprise, her hand stuck fast to the goose and, try as she might, she could not pull it off again.

Presently, the second sister came in, intending to pluck out one of the golden feathers, too. But the moment she touched her sister, she, too, was held fast and could not let go. Finally, the third sister came in for a golden feather. "Keep away! For heaven's sake, keep away!" the other two sisters cried out. However, the third sister did not understand what they meant and thought, "Why should I stay away when they are there?" So she went up to them and touched the second sister's arm and found herself stuck fast in the same way as the others, and so they had to pass the night stuck to the goose.

The next morning, Dummling carried the goose away under his arm and took no notice of the three girls hanging on behind. And wherever he went, they had to follow, and were obliged to run very fast to keep up with him.

In the middle of the field, they met the parson, who, upon seeing the procession, cried, "You bold girls! Aren't you ashamed of yourselves to run after the young man like that? Do you call that proper behavior?"

Then he took the youngest by the hand to pull her away, but no sooner had he touched her than he, too, was held fast and had to run on behind the girls.

Presently, up came the parson's clerk. When he saw the parson running after the three girls, he was amazed and cried, "Hello, Your Reverence! Where are you running off to? Don't forget, we have a christening today!"

He ran up as he spoke, plucked the parson by the sleeve, and found himself stuck fast with the others. As the five trudged along, one behind the other, two peasants came by, carrying hoes. The parson called out to them for help, but no sooner had they touched the clerk than they, too, were held fast, so that now there were seven people running along after Dummling and his goose.

At last they arrived at a town where a King ruled who had only one daughter. This daughter was so thoughtful and solemn that no one and nothing could make her laugh, and the King had proclaimed to all the world that whoever could make her laugh should have her for his wife. Now it happened that she stood at the window of her room as Dummling passed by with his goose and all his train, and when she saw the seven people all hanging together and running madly about, dancing and stumbling and treading on each other's heels, she burst into great fits of laughter and it really seemed as if she could never stop.

Thereupon, Dummling was taken before the King, who gave him the Princess for his wife. The wedding was celebrated, and he became heir to all the kingdom and lived in perfect contentment the rest of his life.

The Four Clever Brothers

"DEAR CHILDREN," said a poor man to his four sons, "now that you are grown up, you must go out into the world and make your own fortunes, for I have nothing to give you. Begin by learning a trade, and see what happens."

So the four brothers took their walking sticks and their bundles of clothing and, bidding their father good-by, went out through the gate together.

After they had travelled some distance, they came to a point where four roads crossed, each one leading into a different country.

"Here we must part," said the eldest brother. "But exactly four years from now, we will meet again at this spot. In the meantime, let us go and try our luck!"

So each brother went his way, and as the eldest was hurrying on, he met a man who asked him where he was going and why.

"I wish to learn a trade," he answered.

"Then, come with me," said the man, "and become a thief."

"No, that is not an honest calling," replied the other, "and where can it lead in the end but to the gallows?"

"Oh, you need not fear the gallows!" said the man. "I will teach you to be so cunning that no one will ever find you out."

So the young man at last agreed to follow his trade, and he soon proved to be so clever that anything he wanted was his for the taking.

The second brother also met a man along the way who asked him which trade he meant to learn.

"I don't know that yet," replied the second brother.

"Then come with me and be a star-gazer. It is a noble trade, for nothing can remain hidden from one who understands the stars."

This idea pleased the second brother very much, and he soon became such a skillful star-gazer that when he had learned all there was to know and was ready to leave, his master gave him a telescope and said, "With this you can see all that occurs in the heavens and on earth, and nothing can be hidden from you."

The third brother met a huntsman, who taught him everything about hunting, and he soon became famous in that trade; and when he was leaving, his master gave him a gun and said, "Whatever you aim at with this, you will be sure to hit."

Meanwhile, the youngest brother met a tailor who offered to teach him that trade.

"I don't think I'd care for that," replied the youngest brother. "Imagine sitting cross-legged from morning to night, working backwards and forwards with a needle and thread!"

"Oh," cried the tailor, "that's not the kind of tailoring I'm talking about. Come with me and you'll learn something quite different and wonderful!"

So the youngest brother was persuaded to learn the art of tailoring from the beginning. When he left, his master gave him a needle and said, "With this you can sew anything together, be it as soft as an egg, or as hard as steel, and not even a seam will be visible to anyone."

Four years passed, and at the time agreed upon the four brothers met at the cross-roads. They welcomed each other joyfully, and then, arm in arm, returned home to their father, to tell him all that had happened to them and how each had learned a trade.

They were sitting under a very high tree in front of the house as they talked, and their father said he would like to put each of them to a test to see if they really were as clever as they said.

He looked up into the tree and said to his youngest son, "At the top of this tree there is a finch's nest. Tell me how many eggs are in it."

The star-gazer took his glass and looked through it. "There are five eggs in the nest," he said.

"Now," said the father to his eldest son, "go up and take the eggs from the nest without disturbing the mother bird who sits on them."

The clever thief climbed the tree and took the eggs from under the mother bird without disturbing her in the least, and brought them to his father.

Then the father put one egg in each corner of the table and the fifth in the center, and said to the huntsman, "Now, cut all the eggs into halves with one shot."

The huntsman aimed, and with one shot struck all five eggs as his father had wished.

"Now it is your turn," said the father to the tailor. "Sew the eggs together again, so perfectly that the shot shall have done the young birds in them no harm."

The tailor took his needle and sewed the eggs as his father wished, and then the thief had to carry them back to the nest and put them under the mother bird without her being aware of it.

She went on sitting on the eggs, and in a few days they were hatched. When the young birds came out, they had only a little red streak across their necks where the tailor had sewn them together.

"Well done!" cried the father. "I don't know which of you deserves the most praise! Let's hope a time will soon come when you will be able to use your talents to the utmost!"

Not long after this, a great outcry arose in the country, because the King's only daughter had been carried off by a dragon. The King was grief-stricken. He mourned day and night and could not be consoled. He issued a proclamation that whoever brought his daughter back to him might have her for his wife.

The four brothers said, "Here is the chance we have been waiting for. Let us see what we can do!"

And they agreed to go together to find the dragon and free the beautiful Princess.

"I'll find out where she is in no time at all," said the star-gazer, and he looked through his glass. He soon cried, "I see her! She is sitting on a rock in the sea many miles from here, and the dragon is guarding her."

Then the star-gazer hurried to the King and asked for a ship for himself and his brothers, and they sailed over the sea until they came to the rock where the dragon was holding the Princess captive. The Princess saw them coming, but the dragon was fast asleep with his head on her lap.

"I dare not shoot," said the huntsman, "for I should kill the Princess as well as the dragon."

"Let me try," said the thief. He crept up to them and took the Princess away from the dragon so quietly and cunningly that the monster did not know it, but snored on.

Joyfully, they hurried with the Princess to the ship and set sail, but the dragon awoke at that moment and missed the Princess. He came flying through the air after them in a great rage, hissing fire, but when he was hovering over the ship, ready to plunge down on them, the huntsman took aim, fired and shot the dragon through the heart.

The dragon fell, but his great weight shattered the ship, and the four brothers and the Princess were thrown into the water. They managed to hold on to a few planks, and these the tailor quickly sewed together with a few large stitches. Then he gathered all the pieces of the ship and sewed them together again so cleverly that in a short time the vessel was ready, as seaworthy as ever, and they sailed home in safety.

They gave the Princess back to her father and there was great rejoicing; and the grateful King said, "One of you shall marry my daughter, but you must settle it among yourselves which of you it shall be."

At this, the brothers began to quarrel. The star-gazer said, "If I had not found out where the Princess was with my glass, all your arts would have been of no use. Therefore, she is mine!"

"But your finding her would have meant little," said the thief, "if I had not taken her away from the dragon. Therefore, she should be mine!"

"No, the Princess is mine," said the huntsman. "If I hadn't shot the dragon, he would have torn you all to pieces."

The tailor said, "And if I hadn't sewn the ship together again, you would all have been drowned. I say she is mine!"

Then the King settled the quarrel, saying, "I wish I had four daughters so that I might give one to each of you, for you are all equally deserving. But since I have only one, none of you shall have her. Instead, I shall give each of you half a kingdom."

"Agreed!" cried the four brothers, for they really did not want to be parted. So the King gave them each half a kingdom as a reward, and they went home, where they lived happily with their father, and took good care of him, for the rest of their lives.